Desert Courage

by
Anne Schraff

Perfection Learning Corporation
Logan, Iowa 51546

Cover Illustration: Carlotta M. Tormey

For information, contact
Perfection Learning Corporation
1000 North Second Avenue, P.O. Box 500
Logan, Iowa 51546-0500.
Tel: 1-800-831-4190 • Fax: 1-712-644-2392

Paperback ISBN 0-7891-5546-x
Cover Craft® ISBN 0-7569-0452-8
perfectionlearning.com
Printed in the U.S.A.
4 5 6 7 PP 08 07 06 05

1 "I don't want to spend the weekend with Dad," Mike Bannon complained to his mother between bites of tuna casserole. "Bruce and I were going to go to the beach with Niki and Tami. We had the whole weekend planned."

"Mike, how much have you seen your father this year?" his mom asked, finishing off a glass of iced tea. "One day at Christmas and a few hours here and there. You're 16 years old. You're almost grown, and you and your father have almost become strangers. That's not right."

Mike had been pretty close to his father before his parents got divorced. One of their favorite things to do together was to go camping. Sometimes they would hike in the mountains and fish from a cold, fast-moving stream. Sometimes they'd ride dune buggies in the desert. Mike's mom didn't enjoy outdoor activities, so she'd go shopping with her sisters when father and son took off for the wilds.

In those days, Mike had felt like the happiest kid ever. But then his dad got promoted in his sales job. He became responsible for teams of salespeople all over the country. Little by little, he disappeared into his work. The job ate him up just as quicksand devours its victims with its shifting form.

It had now been about eight years since Mike's dad and mom split. Now for the first time in a long time, Mike's dad wanted to take off with his son again into the wilderness. But it wasn't the same. Everything had changed.

Two years after the divorce, Mike's mom had married Bob Wilbur. Mike didn't hate him, but he didn't like him either. Mike just ignored his stepdad, which seemed perfectly fine with Bob. He had never wanted children. And after the divorce, it seemed as if Mike's dad didn't want his own child either.

"I don't know what to say to the guy when I see him," Mike told his mom about his dad. "It's real awkward, you know. We just sit there staring at each other. Then I start thinking, when is this going to be over so I can get out of here?"

"He's your father, Mike," his mom said. "He made time for these three days, and you have a school holiday on Monday, so it works out. You need to bond with him, Mike. Really, you do." Even though Mike's mom had asked for the divorce because Mr. Bannon was ignoring her just as he was ignoring Mike, she felt guilty about breaking up the family. She had always believed a boy needed a father, and for a while now Mike really hadn't had one.

"I bonded with him a long time ago, Mom," Mike said bitterly. "You see where it got me. He found something else more interesting than me."

His mom's jaw set in the way it did when she was determined not to take "no" for an answer. "You have got to go on this trip. All these years your father has paid child support. I haven't always made it easy for him to see you, and I have to live with that. But the fact is, he wants this time with you, and you need to respect that."

Mike dropped his silverware on his plate and got up from the table. Without another word to his mom, he marched to his room. He felt like a prisoner on a chain gang. His dad had bought a new sport-utility vehicle, and he had called a week ago about the trip. He had sounded as excited as he used to sound when he and Mike headed out to the wilderness.

"We'll have a great time, Mikey," he'd said enthusiastically.

Mike had winced. His dad hadn't called him "Mikey" since he was eight years old. Mike did not appreciate it now. About a year after the divorce, Mr. Bannon had married a woman named Debbie with a six-year-old son. Over the years Mike had seen her and the skinny, pale kid maybe three or four times. The kid, Ryan, was always clinging to his mother like a baby, and Mike instinctively disliked him. The woman was slim with dark hair and dark eyes. She was sort of pretty, but not nearly as pretty as Mike's mom—in Mike's opinion, anyway.

Mike blamed his father for the divorce. He had shut out his family. Mike had seen his mother crying from loneliness. He had cried too. His dad's excuse was always the same. *I am working so hard for you. I am slaving away so my wife and son can have a better life. Why can't you see and appreciate that?*

The SUV pulled into the driveway after sundown on Friday. Mike's dad said they would be driving into the desert at night and would reach the campsite around midnight. Then they could wake up to a desert sunrise.

"You're in for a treat," he promised. "In April the desert is perfect. It's blooming with flowers, and it's usually not too hot yet."

Mike grimly filled his backpack and walked sullenly out to the SUV after saying good-bye to his mother. His mom and dad had a friendly conversation. For just a few crazy moments, seeing them smiling and laughing together made Mike think maybe the good old days were back and they could be a family again. But, of course, that was a fantasy, and Mike did not believe in fantasies anymore.

As Mike climbed into the front seat of the SUV, he spotted the skinny kid in the back, his face broken out in acne.

"Hey," Ryan said, smiling over braces on his teeth.

Mike didn't even greet the other boy. This was too much. Mike climbed out of the vehicle and glared at his father. "You never said *he'd* be along. You said you and I were going camping. What's with this?" he said angrily.

"I know, Mikey, but at the last minute, I couldn't see why Ryan couldn't tag along. I thought you guys might hit it off and—" his dad said, looking guilty.

"Don't call me Mikey, okay?" Mike snapped. "I don't want to go on this trip."

"Please, Mike," Mr. Bannon said in the most pathetic tone of voice Mike had ever heard from him. He looked old too, much older than his 45 years. "Just do this for me. It's only going to be three days. Please be a good sport about it, for old time's sake."

"Did Mom know Ryan was coming along?" Mike demanded.

"No, she didn't know," his dad said. "Mike, it'll be okay. It won't be so bad. Ryan is a good kid. You guys will get along fine."

Mike was so angry, he wanted to walk

back into the house, go to his room, and slam the door. But something desperate in his father's eyes stopped him. So Mike swore under his breath, threw his backpack in the SUV, and got in.

Ryan, still stretched out in the backseat said, "Hey, dude, I don't like this any better than you do. I'd rather be home watching wrestling."

Mike ignored him as the SUV backed from the driveway.

"Remember when we went camping in the desert about—what? Eight years ago, or nine?" Mike's dad asked.

"I don't remember," Mike said, though he did. It had been nine years ago, when Mike was seven. They had camped in the Anza-Borrego desert in California.

"I hate camping," Ryan said. "I'd rather be home watching TV or playing on the computer."

"You do too much of that, Ryan," Mr. Bannon said. "It's time you learned to appreciate the great outdoors. Mike can tell you how much fun we had camping, hiking, and fishing in the mountains. Weren't those great days, Mike?"

"I don't remember," Mike said stubbornly, though he remembered each trip in all its details. He knew he was being a pain, but he didn't care. This trip wasn't his idea. His mom had forced him. And if he had known beforehand that that geek Ryan was part of the deal, not even his mom could have gotten him to go.

"We'll be seeing a lot of wildflowers," Mike's dad continued, ignoring Mike's bad mood. "We had a wet winter, so we should be in for quite a show. Some of the cactus get these delicate pink and yellow blossoms."

"It's windy out there," Ryan grumbled. "We won't get a sandstorm, will we? Look, the wind is even blowing around here. And what about snakes?"

"Oh, we'll have to watch out for rattlesnakes, right, Mike?" his dad asked with a friendly smile toward his son. Mike could tell he was trying to coax warmth from him, but it was awkward and strained. He remembered hanging out with his dad when he was little, and it was always comfortable and fun. Mike always thought he had the best dad in the world. He was as much fun as a kid, but he was a dad too, and he was always there to protect Mike. So Mike wasn't afraid to take a few risks.

Over the past eight years, Mike had had quite a few fantasy conversations with his father, trying to resolve the hurt he felt.

Dad, was your job worth it? I mean, looking back on it now, how it broke up your marriage, how you lost me . . . was it all worth it?

Mike imagined his father always trying to weasel out. *Mike, I never thought being ambitious and wanting better things for my family would lead to what happened. I wanted you guys to have the best. Was that a crime? And then, when your mom wanted out, I tried to keep us together, you and me. But then I got transferred to Chicago, and what could I do?*

You didn't have to go to Chicago, Dad.

Mike, it was the opportunity of a lifetime, his dad would say, looking sad and guilty. And then Mike would always feel a little better because he'd hurt his father like he had been hurt.

But Mike never had that conversation with his father in real life. Maybe, he thought, he would at last be brave and mad enough on this stupid trip to have that showdown with his father.

As they neared the desert, Ryan opened the window in the back of the SUV. Then he began whining to his stepfather. "You said it'd be cool, but the air seems really warm."

As the sagebrush began to appear outside the windows of the SUV, Mr. Bannon said, "If it's too warm, we'll just camp overnight and then go on into the mountains."

It was dark now. Stars began coming out like little campfires in the sky.

"Remember, Mike, when you were little, and we'd sit on rocks in the desert and watch the stars come out?" his dad asked, stealing glances at the night sky. "And we'd name them. You named them after cartoons you were watching on TV. Remember?"

"Yeah," Mike finally said. He couldn't keep on lying that he didn't remember. But he was in no mood to reminisce about the good old days before the divorce. It hurt too much. Mike remembered turning nine right after his dad moved out and feeling totally alone and crying himself to sleep.

His dad hadn't even made it for Christmas that year.

You abandoned me, you jerk, Mike thought. Didn't you ever think about me and how I felt? Didn't you ever think about that little boy who wanted his dad so much? Didn't you *care*, even a little?

But once again, Mike left his thoughts unsaid.

"This road is bumpy," Ryan complained after they left the main highway and continued the journey on a road that was no more than tire tracks. "You sure we should be driving here?"

"It's okay," Mr. Bannon said. "This road will take us to the best place to camp. The SUV can handle rough terrain. Remember, Mike, when we'd go places in that old jeep? Boy, she could go anywhere."

Mike ignored his father's question. He was tired of traipsing down memory lane.

"I wish we were going to stay at a hotel," Ryan said. "I'd have liked it better if we'd gone to Las Vegas."

"You've been to Las Vegas a dozen times," Mr. Bannon said. "I'd think you'd be tired of it, Ryan."

"It's always fun there," Ryan said. "You ever been, Mike?"

"Yeah. I hated it," Mike said. "It's so fake."

"You're nuts, Mike," Ryan said, laughing. "I never met anybody who wasn't crazy about Vegas."

Mike thought that if Ryan were in his school, he'd be one of the kids he'd avoid. He wouldn't be mean to him or anything, but he wouldn't be friends with him, either. Ryan was weird. How strange it was to think that for the last eight years his dad had played father to this weird kid who wasn't even his own boy. And all the time he was ignoring his own son. What kind of man would do that?

Mike begrudged Ryan all those times he sat across the dinner table from Mike's dad and listened to his corny jokes. It was wrong. It was unfair. Mike knew it wasn't Ryan's fault, but he still held it against him. He couldn't help it.

Mike thought he'd be so glad when this stupid trip was over. He resolved to get out of any future trips at all costs. The next time his father wanted time with him, Mike decided he'd give him a taste of his own medicine.

Mike would just be too busy.

The road got even rougher. The SUV was bumping up and down, and Mike's dad had to slow down to keep control of the vehicle. "Aren't we ever going to get there? I'm sick to my stomach," Ryan whined.

"Just a little bit yet," Mr. Bannon said. "I'm heading for this really neat cavern with a little stream and a waterfall. Mike and I camped there once. I think it was the year Mike turned seven. Right, Mike?"

"I guess," Mike said.

"I remember we named it 'Mike's Cave,' " his dad said.

Suddenly, without warning, the SUV gave a terrible lurch. Ryan screamed as the big vehicle tottered on its side for a moment, then plunged another 20 feet into a ravine, landing on its roof.

Mike was so shocked, he didn't even know what had happened. All he knew was that they were upside down, and the inside of the SUV was filled with dust. Ryan continued to scream, and the awful sound filled up the dark chasm they had fallen into.

"Daaaad!" Ryan sobbed.

2 "Shut up!" Mike yelled at Ryan. Mike freed himself from his seat belt and looked around. "Everybody okay?"

"Yeah," his dad said. Mike turned toward his dad. The door was caved in on the driver's side, and there was a look of pain on his dad's face.

"We're trapped!" Ryan cried, trying and failing to open the side door. "The door's jammed against something!"

Mike crawled over the roof and tried all the doors, but the SUV had fallen into a rocky crevice. None of the doors would open.

Gotta keep calm, Mike told himself. We'll get out of this thing. Just need to keep cool . . .

Mike tried the button that opened the windows, but nothing happened. The vehicle had all power windows. There were no manual controls.

"Can't open the windows without the engine going," Mike muttered.

"So turn the engine back on," Ryan yelled.

"No!" Mr. Bannon shouted as he crawled beside Mike. "I think I smell gasoline. A spark could turn this thing into an inferno!" It was clear that his dad's leg had been hurt from the way he dragged it.

"What's wrong with your leg?" Mike asked.

"I just twisted it some. It's okay," his dad said quickly, but Mike noticed that there was blood on his pants.

"The back hatch," Mike cried, scrambling for the back of the SUV. He grabbed the inside lever and sprung the door open, letting in a gush of cool air. It had gotten cooler the closer they got toward the mountains. The sight of the brushy landscape and the sky swept Mike with relief. For a few horrible moments he had thought they would not be able to escape the SUV, even if it started burning from a ruptured gas tank. "Come on! Everybody out!" he shouted.

Ryan came first, followed by Mike's dad, who moved very slowly and painfully.

"Where's the cell phone?" Ryan asked. "We can call for help right away."

Mike and his father exchanged looks. The last Mike saw of the cell phone, it was lying on the dashboard. Now it was anybody's guess where it was. In the violent turmoil of the accident, the phone probably slipped into some corner of the overturned SUV.

"I'll crawl back in and look for it," Mike volunteered. His dad was unable to climb into the wreck with his injured leg, and Mike knew Ryan was afraid to go into the SUV with the heavy smell of gasoline.

Mike scrambled into the back of the vehicle and quickly snatched up items. Most of the contents of the SUV now rested on the ceiling of the vehicle. He tossed the three backpacks out into the ravine, followed by the ice chest. The backpacks were precious with their contents of trail food, water canteens, and first-aid items. The ice chest contained some sodas and a priceless bottle of water.

Mike found a flashlight and used it to search for the cell phone, but he couldn't find it. He did find the sleeping bags, though, and tossed those out.

"Got 'em," Ryan shouted.

"Found the cell phone yet?" his dad asked.

"Not yet," Mike answered, sweeping the inside of the SUV with his flashlight.

"You gotta find it," Ryan pleaded. "We're stuck in the middle of nowhere. We have to get help!"

Mike continued searching every nook and cranny of the inside of the vehicle until at last his fingers closed around the shattered pieces of plastic that once enclosed the cell phone. In their mad rush to escape, one of them had stepped on the phone and crushed it. It was now a useless tangle of crushed batteries and wires.

Mike crawled from the SUV with the wreckage of the cell phone in hand. "It's smashed. The cell phone is smashed," he said.

"Smashed?" Ryan cried. "It can't be! What'll we do?"

"Somebody stepped on it and crushed it," Mike said. "Nothing we can do about it now."

"Dad, what're we gonna do?" Ryan yelled.

Mike stiffened. Dad? *Dad*? Where did Ryan get off calling Mike's father "Dad"? He wasn't Ryan's father. Where did that come from?

"It'll be okay, Ryan," Mr. Bannon said. Mike thought back to the times he and his father had run into problems on their camping trips. His dad always assured Mike that everything would be fine, and it was. Of course, Mike had been a young boy then. To him, his father was a giant and a miracle worker. Mike had believed that nothing in the universe could hurt him as long as his dad was there. When the boat overturned on the stormy lake, Mike clung confidently to his father, and they safely reached the shore. But this accident was the worst that had ever happened.

"Let's get out of this ravine," his dad said, limping up the sloping cliff.

"Where are we anyway?" Ryan asked. "Do we know where we are?"

"I haven't got my bearings yet," Mr. Bannon said. "I think we're about a mile from that cave." He stopped and stared at the place where the road had collapsed. "I guess the road washed out in those big winter rains. I just never saw what was ahead . . ."

"There should've been a sign if the road was gone," Ryan said.

"We were traveling on a dirt road," Mike's dad pointed out.

He walked to a rock, sat down, and rolled up his pant leg. Mike could see that his calf was badly bruised and cut slightly. But Mike figured the worst damage had been done when he had twisted his leg and pulled a muscle. Mike could tell that his dad couldn't walk at all without great pain.

Mike glanced around the landscape. It looked like pictures he had seen of the moon—rugged, desolate, and forbidding. There were distant, ragged outlines of mountains and a great expanse of sand. Mike remembered camping on the desert before and how he'd loved the experience. The stars had seemed so close. The whole world had seemed to belong to them, to Mike and his dad. But everything was different now.

"We might as well just camp here for the night," his dad said.

"Here?" Ryan groaned. "In the middle of nowhere?" It was the second time he'd called this place "the middle of nowhere." Mike glanced at the slender boy. He looked young for his age. He looked about 12, not 14. Probably the most exciting thing he'd ever done before this was camping out in his own backyard.

Mike's dad instructed the boys to spread out their sleeping bags on the sand. Then Mike dug in the backpacks and found some nutrition bars. They each ate one and drank a can of soda. It didn't quench their thirst as much as water, but they needed to use up the soda before it got hot. They knew the little bag of ice they brought wouldn't last long, especially when the heat returned the next morning.

"Don't worry, Ryan," Mr. Bannon said, reaching over and grasping the boy's hand. "We'll look back on this and laugh about it as one wild adventure. We didn't get hurt in the accident. That's the important thing. We can get another vehicle. Just try to sleep, and tomorrow we'll find a way out of here."

"What if a rattlesnake comes along and crawls in my sleeping bag? What if it bites me, and I get poisoned and die?" Ryan demanded.

"Rattlesnakes don't just come along and bite people for no reason," Ryan's stepfather said. "They strike when they feel threatened. Anyway, we're in open country, and they tend to hang around rocks. Isn't that so, Mike?"

Mike was tempted to say he didn't know. He resented Ryan too much to want to reassure him. Ryan had enjoyed all the love and companionship that belonged to Mike over the past eight years. But grudgingly, Mike said, "Yeah."

Even though he was the most frightened of the three, Ryan fell asleep first. Mike heard his even breathing, indicating he was asleep. But Mike's dad was still awake. Mike turned and looked at his father. "Your leg bothering you?" he asked.

"It aches a little, but it's okay," he said. "I wrenched my leg a few years back playing tennis, and every time I aggravate it, it gives me heck."

Mike swallowed and then asked a question he'd been thinking about ever since the trip began. "You been camping with Ryan before?"

"No," his dad said.

"How come?" Mike pressed the question. He and his dad used to go camping every chance they got in the old days. "You always said it was your favorite thing. How come all of a sudden you stopped?"

There was a long silence. Everything was so quiet there that even the silence seemed to have a sound of its own, a breathy hum. Mike thought maybe it was the wind through the dry canyons.

"It wasn't fun anymore," his dad said simply.

"I never went again either," Mike said. "Uncle Thad wanted to take me when he went with my cousins, but I never went."

"Yeah," his dad said softly.

So there it was, the sad truth. The camping trips had been fun because Mike and his dad were such great companions. When there was no more "Mike and Dad," the fun ended too.

Mike wanted to ask more, but he didn't. He had a lump in his throat. He thought he had put the pain behind him, leaving just a residue of dull anger. But the pain was still so fresh after all this time. The questions still burned his soul like acid.

Why did you go away and leave me, Dad?

Why didn't you find a way to be with me, even after the divorce? Why didn't you move heaven and Earth to be with me? I would have done anything to be with you, but I didn't have the power. You and Mom had all the power . . .

The unearthly wail of an animal in the distant hills pierced the night silence. Ryan popped up in his sleeping bag. "What's that?" he demanded, his eyes wild.

"Just coyotes," Mr. Bannon told him. "Don't worry about them. They don't bother people."

"But they're like wolves, aren't they?" Ryan asked, not willing to be consoled. "They travel in packs like wolves, don't they? And they run down their prey."

"They're not like wolves," Ryan's stepfather said patiently. "They don't attack people like wolves. Go back to sleep, Ryan."

The long, drawn-out wails of the coyotes gave way to short yipping barks. "They sound so freaky," Ryan said with a shudder. "What do they eat?"

"Just mice and things like that," Mike's dad said.

"Sometimes they eat antelope and deer," Mike said. His dad turned and gave him a critical look. Mike knew it wasn't good to scare Ryan even more with that kind of information, but he didn't care.

"If they eat antelope and deer, then how come they don't eat people?" Ryan demanded, his fear rekindled.

"Maybe they do, but there's not much we can do about it," Mike said. "They'll probably find something else to eat before they come down here. Let's hope for that."

"Mike!" his dad scolded. He didn't usually use that harsh tone of voice. It always meant that he was annoyed and was demanding attention. Mike used to pay a lot of attention to it, but now he didn't care.

Mike listened to the wailing of the

coyotes and their barking. He didn't care if his father was disappointed in him. His dad could never be more disappointed in Mike than Mike had been disappointed in his father.

3 With the first shock of the accident wearing off, Mike thought, how bad could this be? When daylight comes and we get a fix on where we are, we'll just hike to the nearest civilization. There's probably a ranger station or some gas station or something nearby. It's only April. The heat won't be too bad. It's not like the middle of August or September when the heat gets really bad. We've got enough food and water for a couple days.

Mike slept fitfully through the night, but he was awake before the dark sky was streaked with even a hint of dawn. He climbed from his sleeping bag and snapped on his flashlight, walking to the ravine where the SUV lay.

Mike could see that the vehicle was crammed between two granite boulders. That's why they couldn't get the doors open. The road they had been traveling on had apparently given way during a winter cloudburst. It was understandable how the accident had happened.

Mike crawled into the ravine to retrieve a bag of charcoal from the vehicle. By the time he was getting the bag from the SUV, there was a faint glow of dawn in the sky. Mike got his first good view of the SUV now, its shiny, new body bruised and bent in the accident. His dad made really good money, so he had bought the best sport-utility vehicle on the market. Now it looked like something in a wrecking yard.

His dad always excused his long hours of work by pointing to the things he could now buy for his family. When his mom pleaded for him to work shorter hours, he'd say, "I want the best college for Mike and other kids we might have. I want a nice house, nice cars, nice furniture. I owe my family the best possible life. I want us to have a great retirement when that time comes. All that costs money. Working hard now will reap benefits for the future . . . "

But there was not to be a future, not for Mike's parents. There would be no other kids, and there would be no retirement together.

Mike carried the charcoal up from the ravine and got a fire started on the grill they had brought. When the blue flames died down and the coals were red, he put coffee on.

It must have been the smell of the coffee that roused his dad and then Ryan.

"How's your leg this morning?" Mike asked.

His dad winced and forced a smile. "I'll be okay," he said. He glanced skyward. "Looks like a beautiful desert sunrise. Your first desert sunrise, huh, Ryan?"

"Who cares?" Ryan whined. "We're stranded here for who knows how long, and we don't know what's going to happen, but I should care about a stupid sunrise?"

Mike poured three cups of coffee. His mom always said that hot coffee made any problem you had to deal with less formidable. Looking back on his childhood days before the divorce, Mike thought his parents were so great together. They always seemed so happy, laughing together and kidding around.

How did it all happen? How did it all go wrong?

Mike couldn't see what his mother saw in her second husband. Bob Wilbur was an accountant, a quiet man without a sense of humor. But he was always home on weekends and was very attentive to Mike's mom. That had to be the draw. Bob didn't want children, but he tolerated Mike about as well as Mike tolerated him.

As Mike's dad drank his coffee, he unfolded a detailed map of the region that he had drawn by hand before starting out. He based it on real maps and trips he had taken in the area. "Now let's see where we are," he said. "See, here's where we cut off the main highway and started down the dirt road. How far do you figure we came?"

"We'd been driving for about 45 minutes," Mike said. "Doing about 35, don't you think?"

"So maybe we came 25 miles," his dad said, worry underscoring his eyes.

"Maybe we were doing 30," Mike said. "That'd be more like 20 miles."

"That puts us pretty far from anything," his dad said. He tugged at his T-shirt. "And

I haven't listened to the weather reports for the past couple of days, but it feels like it's going to be a lot warmer than it should be in April . . ."

The sun was a red ball in the sky, rising from behind the wall of mountains. Mike could feel the cool of the night fading rapidly.

"Yeah, it's gonna be hot," Mike said. "Probably a scorcher. It's almost May. In the desert it can get awfully hot sometimes in May."

Mike remembered one spring when they'd camped in the desert and it had grown extremely hot. They quickly broke camp and headed for the mountains and cooler weather.

"No shade around here," Mike said, frying strips of bacon they had brought. They put them on bread for breakfast.

"We'll be fried alive, just like that bacon," Ryan said. The sun was swelling as it bounded into the sky.

Mike had never paid much attention to the sun before, but now he stole furtive glances at it. It had become an enemy, an evil monster that planned to cook them with its fiery rays.

"We'll have to find some shade, that's for sure," his dad said. "According to this map here, we should be within walking distance from that cave. It would be a perfect place to stay. There's even an all-year spring in the cave."

Mike had been a little kid when they'd dubbed the cavern "Mike's Cave." He had no idea where it was. His dad's map showed only rough estimates of distances. But his dad was determined that the cave was close. "I remember walking along the dirt road. Pretty soon there were some giant saguaros, and then the cave was right there," he said.

"You think you can make it, Dad?" Mike asked.

"Oh yeah, sure. There's an old umbrella in the SUV. If you get it for me, Mike, I can use it as a walking stick to lean on. It should do just fine," his dad said.

Mike went back to the wreck and retrieved the umbrella. It was about three feet long and had a curved handle, just like a cane. Mike handed it to his dad. He took it, smiling. "This is perfect," he said.

"This is Debbie's umbrella. I'm sure glad she put it in the SUV."

Debbie was Mr. Bannon's second wife. Mike resented the way his dad smiled when he spoke her name, as if he loved her a lot. Mike wanted him to still love his mom, but of course that was foolish. His mom didn't love his dad anymore either. She loved Bob.

Weird, Mike thought, how parents stop loving each other and get divorced, and then start loving someone else. It's like you don't like your sweatshirt anymore, so you toss it and get another favorite sweatshirt. It's too bad, Mike thought, that it doesn't work for kids like that. It's too bad kids can't switch their love on and off. Instead they get stuck loving people who have been replaced.

"Well, let's go find Mike's Cave," Mike's dad said, trying to sound lighthearted. He winced with every step he took though, in spite of the fact that he was using Debbie's umbrella for support.

"I bet we won't find the cave," Ryan said. "The sun is getting hotter every minute. I bet we get stuck out here in the broiling heat and there's no cave to be found."

"If we feel it's getting too hot and we haven't found the cave yet, we'll double back," Mr. Bannon promised. "We won't go so far that we can't make it back to the ravine. If worse comes to worst, we can huddle in the shade the vehicle is casting."

"I read somewhere that if you get lost in the desert, you should stay with the vehicle anyway because the searchers usually find that," Mike said.

"In this case, the cave would be a better bet," his dad insisted. "With the sun beating down on the SUV, it'd be impossible to stay inside it. I figure we'll come to the cave quickly. I know that there's a little gas station about eight miles north of the cave. So with any luck, we can rest in the cave for the day and have our fill of water from the springs. Then when night comes, you guys could walk to the station and get help."

The trio wore baseball caps, but the caps were little protection against the brutal sun. Mike noticed his father's limp growing worse as they walked across the sand. It was windy too. The desert winds often kicked up furiously. Mike knew it was no small thing to be caught in a sandstorm.

"You sure you're okay to keep walking?" Mike asked his father nervously.

"Sure, no problem," his dad said gamely. Mike knew his dad was in pretty good shape. He had always been a walker and a runner, though he was heavier now than when he had been married to Mike's mom.

"What if we get heatstroke and die?" Ryan asked, melodramatic as ever.

"Come on, Ryan, don't always expect the worst," Mr. Bannon said. "We'll be there before we know it. Look at those saguaros in the distance. I could be wrong, but they look like the stand I remember seeing near the cave."

Ryan stopped walking and took a big gulp of water from his canteen.

"Don't drink it all at once, man," Mike snapped. He was getting very sick of Ryan and his whiny attitude. Now he was getting careless too. "We might need every drop of water we have to survive. We didn't tell anybody exactly where we were going, so it might take a long time to find us."

"See," Ryan cried, "Mike doesn't believe we're gonna find the stupid cave either. He thinks we're gonna be stranded out here with no water for weeks!"

"I didn't say that," Mike said, turning and staring at Ryan. His patience was nearly gone. "It's just that you have to prepare for the worst. We can't be gulping down water like we've got gallons of it. There's a half-filled jug of water back at the ravine and what's in our canteens, and that's it."

"Mike is right. We have to conserve water," his dad said.

Ryan gave Mike a dirty look and started walking after his stepfather again. They walked past the saguaros Mr. Bannon had seen in the distance, but there was no cave in the rocky outcropping of rocks.

"I bet we're going in the wrong direction," Ryan said.

4 "I could swear the cave was right around here," Mike's dad said, frowning. "Of course, it's been a long time since I was here. I suppose I could be mixed up . . ."

"I wish we hadn't come on this stupid trip," Ryan said. "Why did we have to go camping? Mom said it wouldn't work. Remember? She said Mike was too old to want a father now. She said Mike and I were strangers, and we wouldn't want to be together on a camping trip. And that's true! Why did we have to do this?"

"Whining won't help now," Mike said.

As he walked, Mike thought about what Ryan had just said. His dad was making this big desperate effort to reclaim the son he had neglected. He thought it would be more likely to happen on a camping trip. He thought Mike would remember all the other wonderful camping trips, and somehow all the loneliness and the hurt would vanish in the warm glow of togetherness. Mike had long since gotten rid of his fantasies. But it looked like his dad still entertained his.

"Mike doesn't want a brother, and I don't either," Ryan continued wailing. "Why did we do this? Now look, we're probably gonna die out here. They'll find our skeletons, bleached white like cow skulls."

Mike stole looks at his dad as they walked. He looked miserable. Mike figured that he had clung to a forlorn hope that on this trip he could not only rebuild his father-son relationship with Mike, but perhaps even the two boys would become friends. His dad knew the family he had with Mike and his mother could never be recovered, but perhaps the two families could do something together. Even if they didn't love each other, perhaps they would like each other, at least a little. Mike knew he especially hoped the boys would bond.

They walked more slowly, their gazes scanning the landscape for any sign of the cave.

"I think we better turn back while we still can," Mike said. "We need to go back to the ravine and rig up some shade. We can use the seat covers of the SUV and the umbrella cloth. It's getting dangerously hot, and the wind keeps kicking up."

Mike's dad looked frantic for a minute, like he was losing it. "I was so *sure* the cave was right here. Listen! Don't you hear running water? I'm sure that's the spring . . . If we just go over there where the rocks are—"

"That's just the wind you hear," Mike interrupted, growing tired of his dad's hallucinations. "We've gotta turn back. I'm not kidding. I'm getting sick to my stomach from the heat. This is a crazy spring, dad. It's hotter than I've ever felt it, even in summer. We've gotta go back, or we could die here."

The trek back to the ravine where the SUV rested was exhausting. Mr. Bannon's leg was growing worse, and Mike feared he wouldn't make it at all and the boys would have to carry him. Mike wasn't sure he and Ryan could carry the heavy man all the way back.

Mike thought how wrong he had been about his father in so many ways. He had thought his dad was a skilled outdoorsman, but he was really unskilled. He had driven the SUV into the ditch by not paying close enough attention to road conditions.

Back when he was a small boy, Mike had thought his dad was Superman. But now, in retrospect, Mike could see how many bad mistakes his dad had made, even then. They almost drowned in a lake because his dad had ignored an oncoming storm. One time they tumbled down a steep, icy cliff. But his dad had always made things right in the end, and Mike loved and admired him too much to see his errors.

But now Mike saw it all clearly, the great flaws in his father. In fact he saw little that was good. The man was foolish and ignorant about simple precautions. But then, what could you expect from a man so blind that he did not see his whole family disappearing before his eyes?

As they walked, Mike kept stealing nervous glances at his father. He looked terrible, as if he might have a heart attack and collapse before they got back to the ravine. And if that happened, what could be done? Nothing. Mike and Ryan could only stand and watch him die.

"You doing okay?" Mike asked his father. "You want to rest?"

The heat was like spears driving themselves into the trio's spines and through their brains.

"I'm okay," his dad said, scarcely above a whisper.

Ryan walked beside Mike, a little behind his dad. "He's not going to make it, is he?" Ryan sounded near tears.

"Sure, he's going to be okay. We're almost there," Mike said. He didn't think he'd be this scared that his father was going to check out. He didn't think he had this much feeling left.

Another thing he was wrong about.

They finally reached the ravine. By this time Mike's dad could barely take a step. Mike helped him down beside the SUV. There was enough shade to escape the sun's direct rays. He sank down and slowly sipped some water. He closed his eyes and trembled a little.

For the first time since the accident,

Mike wondered if they would make it out of there alive. If they *all* would make it. If *any* of them would make it.

Mike recalled bits and pieces of news stories he had heard over the years about people lost in the desert. Some were desperate people from Mexico crossing the border in search of jobs to feed their families, but they were stopped by the relentless sun and the unforgiving desert. Their bodies would be recovered in pitiful little heaps where they huddled in the scant shade of shrubs. Or else the desert's victims would be travelers like Mike, his dad, and Ryan, fools who'd gone out for an excursion and ended up dying in their frantic effort to get back to civilization. They had not been smart enough to fear and respect the desert. They saw it as a silly playground, like the theme parks where all the dangers were contrived.

Mike got a sharp knife from his backpack and cut the seat covers out of the SUV. The army knife he'd gotten from his Uncle Thad one Christmas had never come in handier. Using the cloth from the seat covers and the umbrella, Mike created a pool of shade large enough to shelter them all beside the vehicle. He attached one end to the underside of the vehicle and the other to several stout shrub stalks.

"Dad, you look pretty beat. You better rest until the sun goes down," Mike said. He turned to Ryan then. "I was thinking we could write a message in the sand up there in the open country, like a call for help. I mean, if a private plane saw it, if it flew low enough, we might get lucky."

Ryan stared at Mike. "How do we write a message in the sand?" he asked.

"Rocks," Mike said. "We can find some darker rocks and form the word 'help' as big as we can make it so it could be read by a low-flying plane. Guys are always flying around up there."

"You mean we're supposed to drag rocks around in this heat?" Ryan cried.

"You want to be stuck here forever, man?" Mike snapped.

Ryan reluctantly followed Mike to where some rocks lay. Sweating heavily, Mike and Ryan managed to gather enough rocks. Mike arranged them around the word *HELP* that Ryan was writing with a pointy rock he had found. They made the letters large enough that a pilot might just see them. But Mike knew it would take a lot of luck for a plane to be flying low and also scanning the earth below at just the right time.

When they were done with their project, Mike followed behind as Ryan dragged himself to the SUV and collapsed into the shade. Mike's dad was still lying there, resting. The shade provided some relief from the intense sun, but it did not do anything for the sweltering heat. Mike noticed his dad's face was still beet-red, and his clothes were soaked from sweat.

Mike sat down in the shade then, and the three ate nutrition bars and sipped a little water. A plan was forming in Mike's mind.

"You know what, Dad," Mike said in the twilight. "I'm thinking that our only chance is for Ryan and me to walk back down the road we came on. We're sure that road leads to the highway, and if we travel at night, we should be able to get there." Mike was sure his dad would not be strong enough to hike out of there.

"Walk 20 miles?" his dad asked doubtfully.

"It might not be that far," Mike replied. "But even if it is, we could take a rest for ten minutes every hour. We could do it. I just can't think of anything else. The good part of my plan is, we can't get lost. We just follow that road the way we came, and we're sure to reach the highway."

"I can't walk 20 miles," Ryan protested. "Are you crazy? I've never walked more than a couple of miles, and then I got leg cramps."

"Then I'll go alone," Mike said. "I'd rather go it alone if you're going to be whining all the way anyway!"

"No," Mike's dad said, "if anybody goes, you both should. If something were to happen that one of you got injured, the other one would be there to help. You could do it, Ryan. You've got a lot more moxie than you think. You've never tested yourself. You've got to reach way deep inside yourself and find the strong, tough kid who's there."

"I'm telling you," Ryan wailed, "I can't walk that far!"

"And I can't wait for some whining jerk to be convinced," Mike said. He stood up and strapped on his backpack. The sun was going down, and already the punishing heat had lifted. "I'm going!"

"Please, Ryan," Mr. Bannon said, "don't let me down. Your mother is always babying you, saying you can't do sports or much of anything. This is your chance to prove her wrong. This is your chance to prove you're a man, not a weak little boy. This could change your whole outlook on life, Ryan. This is something you could always look back on with pride."

Ryan stood there, looking from Mike to his stepdad. Mike saw fear coursing through his stepbrother. But he thought he could also see a hint of courage. He wasn't sure which was going to win this battle.

"Okay," Ryan said finally, "I'll go. But I'm not saying I'm going all the way. If I see I can't make it, I'm coming back. If I get leg cramps, I'm turning around and coming back."

"Sure, of course," Mike's dad said.

Ryan strapped on his backpack and followed Mike down the road.

"You ever walk 20 miles?" he asked Mike nervously.

"No," Mike said.

"How far have you walked?" Ryan persisted.

"I run five miles a couple of times a week," Mike said.

"But 20 miles is four times that," Ryan said.

"I know, but it's cool. There's a nice, brisk wind. We can stop if we get too tired. Then when we get our second wind, we can go again," Mike said. "The main thing is, we've got to reach the highway before morning. It's not a busy highway, but we should be able to flag somebody down eventually."

"Maybe it's even more than 20 miles," Ryan said. "How do you know it's not 30 miles? That'd be impossible, right? We'd never make that."

"I'm pretty sure it's 20 miles or less," Mike said, irritated. What choice did they have anyway? "At least we can't lose our way and start wandering in circles like some people lost on the desert do. We just need to follow the road we came on."

"You think Dad will be okay? He looked real weak and clammy," Ryan said.

"Yeah, he'll be okay," Mike said.

Ryan seemed to love Mike's dad a lot. That surprised Mike. He wasn't even his real dad.

Mike had sure loved his dad as much as a little kid could before the divorce. And then he was angry and sad, and then, finally, he thought he hated him.

But back there on the trail when his dad looked so bad, Mike realized a lot of the feeling was still there. In spite of anger, he still cared about the guy.

"You ever hang out with your real father?" Mike asked Ryan as they walked.

"Dad is my real father," Ryan insisted.

"No, he's not," Mike said, annoyed. "He's my father, but he isn't yours. He married your mother when you were a little kid, but he's not your father. You got a real father somewhere, and I just wondered if you ever see him."

There was a brief silence. Then Ryan said, "I don't even remember the guy Mom used to be married to. He was mean. I remember that. I was glad when he left.

He scared me. I used to hide under the bed when he was home. I really liked Dad the minute Mom started bringing him home to dinner. Right away he helped me learn to ride my scooter. And he played ball with me and taught me all kinds of things about baseball."

Mike resented hearing all that. He resented thinking of his dad fathering this stranger and forgetting about his own blood. Sometimes Mike wondered if there was something in him that made it easier for his dad to forget him. Was he unlovable in some way? Was there something wrong with him? Mike had asked himself that question many times. But he didn't ask that question much anymore. He had a lot of friends at school and a nice girlfriend. Everybody seemed to like him, from his classmates to the teachers. Still, there was a nagging doubt. How could his dad spend so little time with him if he was such a great guy?

Bitterness swept over Mike as he walked. Suddenly he turned to Ryan and asked, "Did you know about me right from the start, or didn't my father ever talk about me?"

Ryan nodded. "Yeah, he told me right away that he had another son a little bit older than me. He told me he hoped we'd be buddies. He was always saying we'd get together and it would be fun," Ryan said.

"Never happened though," Mike said.

"Yeah, but he was always talking about it," Ryan said. "He wanted us all to go to Europe. I've been to Europe twice, and I went to Japan once. I remember he'd always be saying how great it'd be if his older boy was along," Ryan said.

"Why didn't it happen?" Mike asked, not expecting the kid to know.

"He said a couple of times that your mom wouldn't let you go," Ryan said. "I don't know if that's what happened or not."

Mike's mom had waited two years after the divorce to remarry. His dad was married again in just over a year. Mike was only nine when his mom found out that his dad was getting married again. He remembered her crying all day. She was really hurt. Even though the divorce was her idea, Mike figured she thought his dad would come to his senses and realize he had neglected his family, and maybe then they could get together again. She never really said that, but Mike read between the lines.

Mike figured his mom had fantasies too. Her fantasy was his dad returning to her, apologizing for all the times he wasn't there for her and for Mike. But that fantasy never came true, just like Mike's fantasies never did.

Mike knew that for the first couple of years after the divorce, his mom didn't make it easy for his dad to see Mike. Maybe it was her way of punishing him for how much he had hurt her. She would always schedule doctor or dentist appointments for the days when he was supposed to come to pick up Mike, and then his visit had to be canceled. But Mike never blamed his mother. He knew how much she was hurting.

Mike felt that long before his parents got a divorce, his dad had divorced his mom by staying away so much.

"Did you miss your dad a lot?" Ryan asked, slowing down the pace a little.

Mike's face hardened. "Nah," he snapped.

5 "Didn't you miss him at all?" Ryan persisted.

"I figured if he could get along without me, then I could get along without him. No problem," Mike said.

"Yeah, right," Ryan said.

"What's *that* supposed to mean?" Mike demanded.

"It's just that Dad is such a nice guy. You'd have to have missed him."

"Look," Mike snapped, "he got to be a stranger, okay? My mom remarried, and I got a new dad. He works out just fine, okay?"

As untrue as that was, Mike was determined not to expose his pain to this stupid kid. He didn't need for Ryan to be gloating over what a wonderful dad he had and how sorry Mike must be that he'd lost him.

"How far do you think we've come?" Ryan asked, stopping for a second. He bent over at the waist and put his hands on his knees.

"A mile," Mike snapped, stopping too. "Maybe half a mile." He thought they had covered more distance than that, but he was in no mood to offer Ryan encouraging words. Mike put his hands behind his head and walked around in a small circle, waiting for Ryan to catch his breath. Mike was tired and weak too, but he knew they couldn't afford to stop now.

"A mile!" Ryan gasped. "My feet are hurting already!"

"They'll hurt a lot more before we get there," Mike said. "There'll be blisters on your blisters! Now, let's go!"

They started walking again. Mike walked up ahead. He heard Ryan's sluggish footsteps in the dirt and rocks behind him. He seemed to whimper with every step.

"You really think we can do this, Mike? I mean, walk all this way?" Ryan asked after a few minutes of silence. Mike could tell his resolve was weakening.

"We've got no choice but to try to walk out," Mike said.

"Maybe we should've stayed with Dad at the SUV. I bet somebody would've spotted us," Ryan said.

"Yeah, right," Mike replied. "How many little planes fly low over that desert? Even then, how many pilots are looking down? It's windy, and planes don't even like to fly in this weather. It'd be different if there was a search out for us and somebody had a clue where we were."

"But we were going to call our moms on the cell phone," Ryan pointed out. "They probably know by now something is wrong. When we don't get back Monday, they'll know for sure something went wrong."

"I'm telling you, Ryan, nobody knows where we went. We could have gone to the mountains, down to Mexico, maybe out on a boat. Where are they going to start looking? No, let's face it. Nobody is going to come and rescue us. We have to get out ourselves," Mike said.

"But it's such a long walk," Ryan complained. "My legs are aching already."

"You want to give up? Then the sun will come up, and we'll die of thirst out here. They'll find our dead bodies shriveled up like mummies. Is that what you want?" Mike yelled. He didn't know how much more of this he could take.

"That couldn't happen when we're just 20 miles from civilization," Ryan said.

"Sure it could," Mike said. "People have been found dead one mile from a busy highway. They just never got to it before the heat and dehydration got to them."

"Owwww," Ryan howled suddenly. Mike had seen him stub his toe on a rock that protruded from the dirt road. Ryan stopped to rub his foot. "Owww, that hurts. I hope I didn't break my toe!"

"Watch where you're going," Mike snapped, stopping and turning toward his stepbrother. "Don't be such a baby."

"I need to rest for a minute and look at my toe," Ryan said. "It really throbs." He grabbed the flashlight from Mike.

"Look, man, if we're going to make a big deal out of every little thing, then we'll never make it to the highway before the sun comes up. Forget about your toe, and the pain will just go away!" Mike said.

"I gotta look at my foot!" Ryan insisted, sitting down on a rut in the road and pulling off his shoe and sock. "Look at my poor toe! It's all red. I bet it's going to turn black and blue."

"Okay, fine," Mike said. "You just sit there and look at your sore toe. I'm going on. If some coyotes come down from the mountains and try to lunch on you, well, then that's the breaks of the game. The coyotes hunt at night, you know." Mike didn't really think such a thing would happen, but he wanted to scare Ryan into coming with him.

"Okay, okay," Ryan said, putting his sock and shoe back on. "But if I get an infection and die of blood poisoning, it'll be your fault!"

They kept moving west. The scenery, or what they could see of it in the darkness, didn't change much. To Mike, it felt as if they weren't even moving. Ryan was barely picking up his feet by the time Mike decided to take a break. "We can take five minutes to rest here," Mike said, pointing to a large outcropping of granite. "Take a sip of water. No big gulps, remember."

Ryan sat down and looked at his foot again. "Both my feet are all red and swollen. I'll probably get gangrene," he said.

"That's not how you get gangrene,"

Mike said, taking a small sip of water from his canteen.

Ryan looked resentful. "You think you're so smart. You think you know everything. You're a big jock. You guys make me sick. I hate jocks. The jocks at school are the biggets jerks I ever saw."

Mike turned and glared at the other boy. "How do you know I'm into sports?" he asked.

"Dad has pictures of you plastered all over the house in your stupid football uniform," Ryan said. "I get so sick of looking at your stupid face and your big oaf of a body making a touchdown, or whatever you were doing."

How does Dad come off getting bragging rights? Mike thought. Where did he get off putting up pictures of a son he rarely saw?

But still, it meant something that at least he kept pictures of Mike around his house. It wasn't much, but it was at least a small affirmation that his dad had not totally forgotten him.

"Come on," Mike said then. "Time to get moving again."

"Can't we rest a little longer?" Ryan pleaded.

"No. We've wasted enough time," Mike said. "We've covered just a couple of miles. The going will keep getting tougher, so we've got to make time now. We don't want to be stuck on the road with the sun coming up to roast our brains."

They moved on down the road with Mike trying to pick up the pace a little.

"You're walking too fast," Ryan complained.

"Just keep going," Mike said.

"My feet hurt," Ryan said.

"Don't think about your feet. Think about something else," Mike said, "like girls. Think about the cute girls at school."

"The girls at school don't like me," Ryan said. "They all hang with the jocks. Some of them make fun of me. I don't even like PE 'cause guys make fun of how skinny I am."

"You should go out for some kind of sport," Mike said. "Maybe like karate."

"I'm not getting beat up by people," Ryan said.

"That's not what karate is about. It's real good for building strength and self-esteem," Mike said. "You should look into it."

"I bet you got a million girlfriends. They all love guys who play football," Ryan said. "I bet you get your pick of all the girls. You got a girlfriend?"

"Sorta," Mike said. He didn't really feel like sharing his life with Ryan, but it was better than walking in silence and thinking about how far they had to go. "Her name is Niki. We were supposed to be at the beach this weekend catching the waves, and now look at me—stuck out in the desert!"

They walked through a narrow part of the road where cliffs jutted up on either side. "Hey, look up there!" Ryan said suddenly. "It looks like a spring! Maybe I could go up there and fill my canteen with fresh water. I'd kill for some fresh water."

"That's not a spring," Mike said. "It's just shiny rock, like obsidian. It looks damp, like there's water, but it's like an optical illusion."

"You're crazy," Ryan argued. "I know water when I see it. I can even hear the water running."

"That's the wind. The wind is blowing up pretty good. I hope we don't get a sandstorm," Mike said.

"You think you know everything better than anybody else, don't you?" Ryan said. He walked over to the cliff and felt for evidence of dampness dripping over the stones.

"Stop wasting time," Mike said angrily. "We haven't got time for that. You want to be stuck out here in the sun?"

Ryan trudged on, a few feet behind Mike. They walked for almost an hour before they rested again. Ryan had been complaining nonstop. Now Mike observed that he really looked exhausted.

"I'm telling you," Ryan warned, "I can't keep going like this. We gotta rest more."

"Can't you get it through your thick head that the clock is ticking against us?" Mike exploded. "If we're not even making good time now, what are we going to do when we're *really* tired and we've still got miles to go?"

Ryan got to his feet. "My legs feel like sticks. They're numb. I can't even feel them anymore."

"You shouldn't have come with me," Mike said bitterly. "You should have stayed with Dad. Why didn't you?"

"I did it 'cause Dad wanted me to so much. I wanted him to be proud of me. I wanted him to think I'm as good as you," Ryan said. "He's always talked about you, and I could see how proud he was of you. Dad's been real good to me, but I haven't given him much to be proud of." Ryan's voice wavered with emotion. "He's been such a good dad that I ought to be able to make him proud. My real father was really mean and horrible, and when Dad came along, my life got really great . . ."

"Where's your real father?" Mike asked.

"I don't know," Ryan said. "I never see him. He was in prison."

"What for?" Mike asked.

"For beating on Mom and selling drugs and stuff," Ryan said. Mike got the feeling that there was even more to the story that Ryan didn't feel like sharing, but he let it drop.

"Look, Ryan, if you don't think you can go on, then go back, okay? You can just follow the road the way we came, and you'll be back at the ravine in a couple of hours. I'll go on alone," Mike said.

Ryan's eyes widened. "I should walk back *alone*?" he asked.

You stupid wimp, why not walk back alone? Mike thought. Give me a break! You spineless jerk, just go!

But to Ryan, Mike said, "You can just follow the road back. It's nothing!"

"But what if I get sick or pass out and just lie there, and the sun comes up and burns down on me? There'll be nobody to even know. I passed out once in summer camp," Ryan said.

"What do you mean?" Mike demanded, angry that more time was being wasted. "Are you sick or something?"

"I don't know. Maybe I am. The doctor at summer camp said I'm kinda underweight and . . ." Ryan began to recite his ailments. Mike figured they were all imaginary.

"I don't need this, man," Mike said. "I'm continuing west, Ryan, and if you don't want to keep up with me, I swear I'm leaving you behind. We've wasted almost 15 minutes arguing. Either shut up and come with me or turn back. It's your call."

"Okay, okay," Ryan said. "You go on. I'll go back to the ravine."

Mike nodded. "Good. Just follow the road, okay? You'll be back with Dad long before sunrise."

Ryan walked east, back toward the ravine, and Mike continued west. Ryan walked about three yards before he stumbled and fell. Mike turned and looked at the still form lying on the sand.

Ryan was motionless in the darkness.

6 "Ryan! What's the matter?" Mike shouted, running back toward the inert form on the ground.

Ryan was lying on his back, his eyes rolled back in his head.

"Oh, man!" Mike groaned, kneeling down and shaking the boy. He grasped Ryan's shoulders and lifted him a little. "Ryan, what's the matter? What's wrong?" he shouted.

Ryan mumbled incoherently.

"I can't believe this," Mike said. "Ryan, can you hear me? What's wrong?"

"Wha—" Ryan started to say in a faint voice. "Why's everything look so funny?"

"It's night. It's dark," Mike said. "What happened?"

"Everything's blurry . . . I don't see any color," Ryan said. He looked pale.

Mike had read once that when people faint and then come to, it takes a while for colors to leak back into the world they see. When they first revive, everything is monochrome.

"Are you okay?" Mike asked.

"I don't know. All of a sudden everything got black," Ryan said. He was leaning on his elbows now. "I feel woozy."

Mike swallowed hard. He couldn't leave Ryan alone when he was like this. He couldn't imagine Ryan being strong enough to continue the journey to the highway even when he recovered from the fainting spell.

There was nothing to do but turn back.

The boys walked slowly back, with Ryan stopping often to rest. It was a slower walk back, but by close to midnight, they were back at the ravine.

"Dad," Ryan said brokenly, kneeling by the sleeping bag where his father awakened, "I couldn't make it. I passed out, and Mike had to bring me back. I'm sorry, Dad. I tried, I really tried, but I got sick. I couldn't help it."

Mike's dad sat up, looking from Mike to Ryan. "What happened exactly?" he asked, looking at Mike.

"Ryan kept getting tired and his feet hurt, so we decided he should quit and come back and I'd go on alone. Then he fainted, so I figured I couldn't let him come back alone. I thought he'd maybe faint again," Mike explained.

"Remember, Dad, how I fainted that time at summer camp, and you guys had to come get me?" Ryan asked in a plaintive voice. "Didn't the doctor say I had something wrong with me?"

Mike almost felt sorry for the kid. He was so ashamed of himself, he was making desperate, lame excuses.

"You were only 11 years old then, Ryan, and all that was wrong with you was homesickness," Mr. Bannon said in a frustrated voice.

"I'm sorry I let you down, Dad," Ryan said, seeming near tears.

"It's okay, Ryan. Don't worry about it," his stepdad said. He got out of the sleeping bag and massaged his bad leg. He looked up at the starry sky. "Well, it's too late to make another try at it now. Not to worry though. We still have food and water left. It should last us at least one more day."

"Maybe Mike and I can catch something to eat, like birds or something," Ryan said hopefully, trying to salvage his pride and make himself useful. "We could maybe trap some doves and fry them. One time at camp we ate doves. I think they called them *squab* or something like that. They were good, better than chicken."

"Only birds around here are vultures," Mike said dryly. He wondered if Ryan had had the fainting spell on purpose just so Mike would come back with him and he wouldn't have to make the trip alone. Was he *that* scared? Was he *that* much of a coward? Mike felt nothing but contempt for him.

"You better get some sleep, boys," Mike's dad said. "We have another long, hot day ahead of us. Then tomorrow night we'll see about trying to reach the highway again."

Ryan crawled into his sleeping bag and fell immediately into a deep sleep. Mike built a little fire and made coffee for himself and his dad. He was too tense to go right to sleep, maybe too angry.

His dad cradled the coffee cup in his hand and said, "Be a kick, wouldn't it, if some plane passing over saw our little fire and we got rescued that way."

"Yeah, right," Mike said, "or maybe some aliens will pass by and give us a lift in their spaceship."

Mike was bitterly disappointed. By this time he had expected to be halfway to the highway. He would have been too, except for that cowardly little wimp.

"Mike," his dad said softly, "do you think Ryan really fainted?"

"It looked like it," Mike said, "but I don't know. He could have faked it. He complained the whole time about his feet hurting, his legs aching, being too tired. I thought he'd go back alone, but I guess that scared him." Mike couldn't keep the disgust from his voice.

"He's not a strong boy," his dad said in a sympathetic voice. Mike wondered how his dad could care so much for the little jerk when he didn't mind ignoring Mike for so long.

"Well, it sure messed up my plans," Mike said, taking angry gulps of coffee.

"He had a bad time of it before I married his mother," his dad said.

So did I have a good time of it after you deserted me? Mike thought.

Mike said nothing. He just stared into his coffee and let his father's voice drone on.

"His father abused him," his dad said matter-of-factly. He said it in a low, quiet voice, but it was still shocking to Mike.

"Ryan said the guy beat up on his mom, but he didn't say anything about being abused himself," Mike said.

"He doesn't like to talk about it," his dad said. "But his father would beat him with anything he could get his hands on. His golf clubs, his belt, sometimes his fists. Ryan had four broken arms before he was four, to say nothing of other broken bones."

Mike stiffened. He didn't want to hear this. He didn't want to hear that Ryan had endured far more pain than he had. Mike could not imagine being in a house with a father who would break your bones when you were a toddler. It was almost unbearable to think of such a man.

"Why didn't his mother put a stop to it?" Mike demanded. "How come you married a woman who let something like that happen to her own kid?" Anger surged in Mike's voice.

"Deb came from a home where her father was abusive. She had very low self-esteem. She grew up thinking that's how it was. Don't make your father mad or he's going to hurt you. She's much better now, much healthier. She would accept her husband's stories about the more serious injuries. She knew her husband hit the boy, but she never thought he'd broken bones. The guy convinced her Ryan fell, or was wrestling with other boys, maybe fell off his skateboard. The last time he hurt Ryan, Deb saw it. She grabbed the boy and ran to a shelter. The marriage was over. She pressed charges, and the guy went to prison for a while." Mike's dad told the story in a sad voice.

Mike wondered how his dad could have loved such a weak woman when he had been married to a bright, strong woman like Mike's mom. Mike couldn't ask the question though. Maybe he didn't even want to know the answer. Maybe his dad had been intimidated deep down by someone as strong and vibrant and self-sufficient as his mom.

Maybe *that's* what he'd been running

from when he escaped into his work . . .

"Poor Ryan was a broken-winged little bird when I first met him," Mike's dad continued. "We've tried to mend him and make him stronger, but there are still weak places. I'm really sorry he didn't hang in there tonight with you. It would have made such a difference to him, how he sees himself. I'm so sorry his weaker side won . . . *again*." He sighed deeply and shook his head. "Remember that broken-winged seagull you and I once rescued? How we kept him in a cage? And then one day when he seemed all healed, we opened the cage door, and he wouldn't leave. But the next day, off he went, soaring in the blue sky. I keep hoping that happens someday for Ryan."

Mike remembered the wounded seagull incident, although once again it was a bittersweet memory. He finished his coffee, got up and stretched his legs, and headed for his sleeping bag. Before he got in it, he glanced into the sky and wished with all his heart that a small plane would appear, then circle low, giving evidence that they had seen signs of life.

But that was just another fantasy, Mike reminded himself sternly.

Mike got into his sleeping bag and began to wonder what his mom was thinking right now. She had to be worried that she hadn't received a phone call yet. Last year when Mike got the chance to fly to Spain with his Spanish Club, his mom had insisted that he call her when the plane landed at Madrid. She was strong, but she worried too. Maybe back home she was now so worried that she had already reported them missing.

Not that it would help much, Mike thought. Nobody knew where to look.

Mike's mind continued to churn out memories and analyzations. Lying under the bright stars and moon, it was easy to let his mind wander. Mike's mom's attitude toward his dad had changed in recent years. At first she had been hurt and angry about the divorce. She had blamed his dad for everything. She had tried not to run him down to Mike, but Mike would hear her bad-mouthing him to her mother. "He never should have gotten married. He doesn't know how to be there for a wife and a family," she would say.

Right after the divorce, his mom had seemed glad that Mike had little contact with his dad. At least she didn't care much. When his dad moved to Chicago, Mike's mom had said it was just as well because he wasn't much of a father anyway.

But slowly she changed. It began to worry her that Mike and his father had little more than phone calls and letters. Mike's attitude became embittered and hardened. He didn't enjoy the brief, strained meetings with his father. He sulked through most of the visits. But Mike's mom began to push for him to rebuild something with his dad. That's why she was so anxious that Mike go on this camping trip. She saw it as maybe one last chance for father and son to recover what they had lost before childhood was gone and Mike and his father would be forever strangers.

That's what his mom hoped for, anyway.

But now what was she thinking?

"You sleeping?" Mike asked his father.

"No," his dad answered immediately.

In a way it was easier talking to his dad in the darkness. It was easier not seeing his face. It was almost as safe as talking on the phone. "Why did you keep taking on more and more work when I was a little kid? Why did you work until you were hardly home at all anymore?" Mike asked.

His dad didn't answer right away. When he finally did answer, he came up with the same old excuses Mike had heard before. "I grew up poor, Mike. We, my two brothers and I, didn't have much of anything. Dad couldn't even buy the sports gear we needed to play football. I wanted more for you. It doesn't come easy. You have to work your tail off to have a decent life for your family," his dad said.

"But you were gone almost *all* the time at the end," Mike said. "Did you see that wasn't right?"

Dad took a deep breath. "Yeah, I worried about that. But not a lot. It was fun being the top guy in our department. I felt important. At work I was winning awards, being toasted as 'the man' every time I turned around. It was a heck of an ego trip, Mike . . ." His voice shook a little. "Back home, your mom and I didn't work very much at pleasing each other anymore. I think we both took each other for granted. I thought if I worked hard at my job and the money flowed, everything at home would follow along . . ."

Mike felt a lump in his throat. He couldn't speak.

"I'm sorry, Michael," Dad said. *"I'm so sorry . . ."*

It was the first time in eight years he had said he was sorry.

Mike turned over in the sleeping bag and closed his eyes.

7 During the night, Mike dreamed. He was back home, and his mom and dad were barbecuing in the backyard. Mike must have been seven. His dad burned the steaks. His mom got really angry and yelled at him. His dad yelled something back about her spending too much money shopping with her sisters. Mike hadn't thought anything of it at the time. He was too young. But now he woke up. He realized that his parents used to laugh together a lot, even when one of them made a mistake. But then they didn't laugh so much anymore. That must have been the beginning of the end, he thought. His dad stopped thinking home was more fun than work . . .

The next thing Mike knew, he felt heat on his face. The sun was coming up. It was still early morning but already warm. He got out of his sleeping bag to start coffee. He wished they had gone to the mountains instead and were camped by a cold stream filled with silver fish that could be caught and fried to a crispy brown.

The plan had been to go to the desert for one day, then continue into the mountains. If the SUV had not gone into the ravine, that's where they would be now—in the mountains.

But now the desert heat made Mike feel as if he were standing in front of an open oven door. The heat came blasting at him, driven by a gathering wind. And there was nothing to eat but dry nutrition bars and some jerky.

Mike noticed circling hawks in the sky. He wondered what they tasted like if you could ever catch them. He imagined frying some kind of bird and the tasty, greasy oil drizzling over his lips. He hadn't realized how really hungry he was until now. He wanted to drive to a fast-food place and get a double cheeseburger with bacon on sourdough. He wanted a side of fries and a chocolate shake.

"Look at the big lizard on the rock there," Ryan said. Mike didn't even know the kid was standing there so close until he heard his voice. "Do you think he'd be good to eat?"

"He doesn't look too tasty," Mike said. "I think he'd be pretty tough."

The lizard darted away then, as if he had heard the conversation and wasn't going to stick around.

"Mike!" Ryan cried then. "Do you hear something?"

"What's that?" his dad yelled. "An engine?"

"Yeah," Mike said, "I think it's a plane."

It had to be a private plane. Regular air traffic did not pass over the area where they were. Mike figured some guy was out for a morning jaunt, just cruising the sky.

"How can we get his attention?" Ryan asked.

"Maybe he'll see the help message we wrote with the rocks," Mike said. But he wasn't relying on that. "Let's all grab something and start waving it. If he's low enough, he'll see the action."

Mike began waving an electric blue jacket he had brought along for the chill of the mountains. His dad and Ryan waved the makeshift tarp.

The little plane appeared, like a white bird in the sky.

"How far up do you think he is?" Ryan asked.

Mike's dad had been a pilot in the National Guard. He was pretty good at estimating distances. "Pretty low . . . he's flying pretty low," Mr. Bannon said hopefully.

"Keep on waving the stuff," Mike said. "If he sees something unusual, he'll swing around for a closer look."

"Yeah," his dad said, "he's bound to see flashes of color if he's looking this way. You don't expect to see those in the desert."

But the little plane seemed to be gaining altitude.

"You jerk!" Ryan screamed. "Are you blind?"

"Don't give up," Mike's dad urged. "Keep on waving the stuff. He might be circling for a turn, and then he'll fly lower for a look." But his hope seemed to be waning too.

Mike slowly lowered his blue jacket. "He probably wasn't even looking down this way. It was a long shot anyway."

Mike returned the tarp to its place beside the SUV so it could provide some desperately needed shade. The three of them huddled there, sipping a little water. It was Sunday morning now. They had been there since Friday night. It seemed much longer than that. It seemed they had spent weeks there already.

"Man, it's hot," Mike said. "Seems like the air itself is on fire."

"I hate the desert," Ryan said. "I'm never coming near the desert again when we get out of here. Some people say it's pretty and all that, but all I see is dirty gray sand and ugly, twisted shrubs. We haven't even seen any of those flowers you said would be here, Dad."

"I guess the heat spell wiped them out," Mr. Bannon said. "This is a freak spring. The desert is beautiful when it blooms, but I had no idea this heat wave was on. I never would have come if I'd known."

"Haven't seen any snakes either," Ryan said. "I guess that's good, at least."

The day seemed to last forever. They drank water sparingly and tried to stay out of the unforgiving rays of the sun.

Mike's dad seemed to get weaker. Without much nourishment and water, Mike figured he was getting dehydrated. And his leg was still swollen and turning colors. He didn't say much about it, but Mike knew he had to be in a lot of pain. They had to get out of there—soon.

When the sun began to go down, Mike prepared for his second attempt to walk out to the highway. "This time I'm going to make it," he promised quietly.

To Mike's surprise, Ryan began strapping on his backpack too. "I'm going with you," he announced. "It'll be different this time."

"No way," Mike shouted furiously. "You aren't going with me. You're not pulling that on me twice!"

"I told you it'll be different this time," Ryan said.

"I swear I'll knock you to the ground if you try to come with me, Ryan! This is our last chance! You're not screwing me up again," Mike yelled.

"You can't stop me," Ryan yelled back. "I won't drag you down this time, Mike. It will all be different. Come on!"

Mike turned to his father. "Please make him stay here," he pleaded. "You know what's going to happen. We'll be halfway there, and he'll wimp out on me again. We'll lose our last chance to get out of here alive. If he hadn't messed me up last night, we'd all be out of here having cheeseburgers right now. Dad, make him stay here!"

"Ryan, Mike has a point," Mr. Bannon said. "You're not the athlete he is. He's got a lot more stamina than you have. Stay here with me, Ryan. You holding him back might just be the difference between Mike getting help and failing—"

"So I'm just a hopeless loser, right? I'll never be a man, right?" Ryan cried shrilly.

"Ryan, get ahold of yourself," his stepfather said. "We're just saying that too much is at stake right now. It's better if Mike goes alone. He can make it, but not if he has to worry about you."

"Okay, fine," Ryan said, turning his back to Mike and his father. "Let the big-shot jock go it alone. If he falls into a gopher hole and breaks his leg and there's nobody to help him, he can just dry up and blow away."

"That's not going to happen," Mike said, relieved that Ryan had agreed to stay behind. Mike glanced at his father. "I should reach the highway at dawn, while it's still dark. I'll hail a car, and then help should be here in no time."

"Good luck, son," his dad said.

"You'll be okay here, huh? Got enough water?" Mike asked.

"Sure, we'll be fine," his dad said. But Ryan remained standing there with his back to them. He didn't even turn when Mike once again headed west down the tire track road.

Twenty miles, Mike thought. It sure wouldn't be easy, but he could do it. He planned to make three miles an hour, resting at 15-minute intervals. At that rate, he expected to reach the highway around 3:00 or 4:00 in the morning. He could use his flashlight to help him hail a car. He figured that even if nobody stopped, someone would call for help on a cell phone.

Mike realized that some motorists might be leery of a ragged young guy trying to flag them down in the middle of the desert.

They might think he was some kind of criminal trying to steal a car. Or they might think he was a madman, some wild desert rat. But if they just called the police on their cell phone, everything would be fine.

There was nothing Mike looked more forward to seeing than a police cruiser with its red lights blaring.

Except maybe a double cheeseburger with bacon and fries.

Mike was tempted to jog, but he resisted that urge. He had competed in long-distance races, and he knew you didn't wear yourself out in the early going. You rationed your strength.

Mike walked briskly in a measured step, putting distance behind him. He glanced up at the sky and tried to study the constellations to get his mind on something else. When he was a small boy, his dad pointed out all the constellations. Mike's favorite was Leo the Lion. The bright star Regulus was in Leo's mane, and it was always easy to see. The desert sky was so clear that all the stars were visible, though the wind was kicking up a little now.

The clarity of the cooler nights was a

good thing about the desert, Mike thought. There were precious few good things he felt like saying about the desert right now. The searing heat of the day had sapped his strength. There was a sense of real urgency about this trip. They only had water for about another day, and then they would be in real trouble.

People died all the time during foolish trips into the desert. It could happen. Mike considered the worst-case scenario, failing to reach the highway in time or being forced to return to the ravine. Then what? Hoping another plane came by and spotted them? And if not? By the time the searchers reached them, it would probably be too late.

Mike thought about Niki and how much fun he and she had had the past year. He'd dated plenty of girls, but she was the first girl he really, really liked. She was cute, funny, and very easy to be around. A lot of girls got possessive with guys they liked. A lot of Mike's friends had been caught in those "fatal-attraction-type" situations. But Niki was glad to hang loose and just enjoy the now. She wanted to be a 16-year-old like she was, having a great time, not sinking her hooks into a guy for some big commitment. Neither Niki nor Mike wanted anything major-league.

Now Mike focused his mind on Niki's pretty face, her cute little mannerisms, the jokes she liked to play. When he was with her, they were always laughing.

Mike made good time, his thoughts dwelling on happy things—Niki, his sports teams, classes he was enjoying in school. When he stopped for a rest, he found a large rock that looked like a perfect place to sit.

He sat down and took a small sip of water. He closed the canteen carefully so he wouldn't waste even a drop of the precious liquid. Then he looked around at the distant dark mountains, at the saguaros standing against the sky, their branches lifted as if in prayer.

Mike felt something then. It felt like a pebble in his shoe. He reached down to check it out when he suddenly felt a sharp pain in his hand. When he quickly pulled his hand up, he saw blood coming from his thumb. Mike looked down to see something moving at the base of the rock.

A snake!

Mike turned ice-cold in terror. He hadn't even looked before he sat down on the rock. Snakes often hid under rocks on the desert. Now he'd been bitten!

The large snake slithered off as blood ran down Mike's hand onto his wrist. Panic clutched at him—he'd been bitten by a rattlesnake! The desert was full of rattlers. How could he have been so stupid to sit on a rock without even looking?

Mike remembered reading first-aid instructions in school. If a snake bites you, you make an incision across the bite and suck out the venom as best you can. Then you hurry to a hospital for antivenom serum. But he had no way to get to a hospital!

Mike groped in his backpack for the army knife. His mind was spinning. He was sick to his stomach, and he felt like he was going into shock. Maybe the venom was already paralyzing his nervous system. He was breathing in short rasps.

"Oh, my God," Mike groaned. "I'm gonna die here!"

8 Mike's hands were shaking so badly he could barely get a grip on the handle of the knife. He raised his right hand and tried to make the cut, but the knife fell from his awkward grasp. He stared in horror at the wound, the small break made by the snake's deadly fangs. He was sure the venom was already working its way toward his heart.

Mike finally closed his eyes tight and slashed his hand. He opened his eyes slightly then. It was an ugly knife wound, but he had made an incision in the bite.

Blood streamed out. He poured his remaining water into his wound. Maybe the venom would wash out, Mike hoped. But, no, think! he told himself. He had to remember what he had learned about snakebites. He had to think clearly. His life depended on it!

Thinking back, he remembered reading that you had to suck out the venom. Sometimes you had to suck as long as 40 minutes. You had to keep at it to make sure it was all out, and even then you couldn't be sure.

So Mike brought his bloody hand up to his mouth. He began sucking blood from the wound. He spat the blood and, he hoped, the venom out onto the sand. He felt sicker and dizzier. The blood was salty and sticky. He wondered if he was tasting venom.

What did it taste like?

Mike kept at the job, sucking out the blood and spitting, hoping desperately he was getting the venom before it fatally invaded his body.

Wild thoughts streaked through Mike's brain. How fast does venom travel? Does it rush straight to the heart like an arrow? What really are the symptoms of a fatal snakebite? Does your heart stop beating? If the snake had bitten another animal, would it have used up some of its venom so the next victim got a less dangerous dose? Maybe the rattler had not injected enough venom into Mike to kill him.

Mike stopped sucking the wound for a minute. He was breathing hard, and his mind was erratic. He was only 16. He had so much he wanted to do. Next year he wanted to make it to the state tournament in football. He wanted to experience college life. And then there was Niki . . . True, they weren't serious. But he really liked her. It wasn't fair that he couldn't see how it all turned out.

How could he be dying out in this miserable place from a serpent's bite? he thought, wildly. How could it have happened?

Suddenly something caught Mike's eye. The snake that had bitten him was curled up against a rock about three yards away. He could see it clearly in the moonlight. This ugly thing that had probably taken his life was now taking a nap, Mike thought. It was big, about three feet long. It acted oblivious to the evil it had done.

Mike jumped to his feet. He knew that snakebite victims should avoid unnecessary movement to avoid carrying the venom more quickly to their heart. But he didn't care. He was filled with rage against the ugly, horrible thing that had attacked him for no reason.

"Damn snake," he yelled. He raised the Army knife and cried, "You'll never hurt anybody else, snake!"

Mike raised the knife. He was preparing to plunge it into the snake's head when something stopped him. The snake did not have the diamond pattern of a rattlesnake. When Mike looked closely at the tail, there were no telltale rattles.

Mike was stunned. It wasn't a rattlesnake after all! It had yellow and brown stripes, not diamonds on its body. It was a common nocturnal snake found all over the desert. It had a funny patch on its nose. "It's a stupid patch-nosed snake," Mike cried, remembering his beloved boyhood book of snakes that he read into dust. "It's not poisonous!"

Mike sat down on the sand, rocking back and forth on his heels. "Thank God, thank God," he gasped. Then, out of the blue, he started laughing. He looked at the bloody knife and the horrible wound he had unnecessarily made in his poor hand. He had mangled his hand for nothing. He knew his face was probably streaked with blood from sucking the wound. He felt like a vampire. That thought made him laugh all the harder. He *was* a vampire! He'd sucked blood, hadn't he?

Finally Mike put some antiseptic on the wound and bandaged it from his first-aid kit. Talking to himself made him feel less alone. "Man, what a close call," Mike said to himself. "I could be dead right now." He glanced at his watch. He had wasted 30 minutes, no, 45 at least. But that was okay. He was alive. He had been spared. His stupidity hadn't cost him his life, after all.

Mike had been tired before, but the excitement of his ordeal had sent forth a surge of adrenalin. He felt like he could run a marathon. So he slung on his backpack and continued the westward journey.

His hand felt a little sore, but it didn't bother him. What's a little pain to a vampire? he thought, and began laughing again. He would remember this forever. It would be part of the lore of his life.

Mike kept on walking, feeling no more pain in his wound. Having almost died, or at least thinking he was dying, he now felt rejuvenated, as if now he could overcome anything.

At the end of the third hour since the journey began, Mike stopped to rest again. He didn't sit on a rock this time. He carefully examined a sandy area; then he sat on a small incline. He didn't have any water left, but he was so hungry. So he ate some jerky. He knew he'd probably regret it. The salt of the food would make his thirst even worse. But it would have to go unquenched for now.

He figured he had covered about ten miles already, and his legs were beginning to feel tired. Luckily, he wasn't exhausted yet. He knew he could still go on. He massaged his calf muscles, which seemed to help the fatigue. If he was lucky, he thought he had about ten miles to go. But that was okay. He was not going to dwell on all the miles ahead. He'd just do them, one step at a time. He was going to adhere to his grandmother's advice about how to deal with a long job.

"Take it one piece at a time and then, pretty soon, you're all done, and you're surprised how easy it was."

Mike continued to enjoy the landscape when he resumed his walk. He smiled at the saguaros, noticed the designs of the sand dunes.

And then, about 30 yards behind him, something moved. Mike glanced back and saw it, a shadow. It vanished behind an outcropping of rock. A sense of surprise and then concern came to Mike. Was there some large animal trailing him? What could it be? In the mountains or even the hills, hungry bobcats stalked lone individuals. Mike had never heard of bobcats in the desert, but he wasn't an expert on desert wildlife. A rogue bobcat could have strayed into the desert in a desperate search for food.

A nervous chill ran up his back. He glanced back again, and this time it appeared certain that the creature had ducked. A bobcat wouldn't have done that, would it?

Or maybe Mike's eyes were deceiving him. But it just looked like it had ducked.

Or maybe there was another person out there!

This could be good news, Mike thought. Maybe it was some friendly old desert rat who lived around there. If Mike could reach him, he would probably know a shortcut out of there, or he could get help. He might have an old burro stuck away near his shack. Mike could understand the old fellow being cautious about approaching a dirty-looking young man like Mike who was wandering around in the middle of the night.

Mike started walking again, but he frequently looked back to see if he was being followed. He had walked about ten minutes before he saw the form again. This time he was sure it was a person. It ducked behind a saguaro right after Mike looked.

Maybe, Mike thought nervously, it wasn't some harmless old desert scavenger. What if Mike was the one who needed to be afraid? What if some guy had come into the desert to bury a body or something? But why was he following Mike? Why didn't he just do his dirty work and leave?

What'll I do if he suddenly attacks me? Mike thought.

Mike glanced nervously back again. The distraction was slowing him down just when he needed to make good time.

It was almost midnight, and he wanted to be halfway to the highway by midnight.

Mike slipped behind a heap of rocks and crouched down. He hoped his pursuer would think he had lost Mike in the darkness and then would come hurrying by to look for him.

The form Mike had seen drew closer. It was a man, a slim man. No, not a man—a boy!

"Ryan!" Mike shouted in disbelief.

Ryan seemed about to pop out of his skin when Mike confronted him. "Huh?" he cried.

"Ryan, what are you doing here?" Mike demanded. "You were supposed to stay with Dad. Are you crazy?"

Ryan's face hardened. "I can make it. I'm as good as you are. I told Dad I'd never get over it if I sat and waited and you had to get help for us all by yourself. I wouldn't *ever* think of myself as a man if that happened. So Dad said I could catch up to you and go together like we'd planned before," he said.

"Oh, great," Mike groaned. "This is just what I needed!"

"Just ignore me. Pretend you're still walking alone," Ryan said.

"How can I ignore you when you'll be whining and complaining?" Mike asked bitterly.

"Can't you give a guy a second chance?" Ryan almost screamed. "You're so high and mighty that you never needed a second chance? You never lost your nerve or made a mistake?"

Mike stood there a moment in silence. Then he muttered, "Okay, all right. But you better not slow me down!"

Mike turned and stomped off down the road, still heading west. He figured Ryan was trotting along behind him. He wouldn't say so, but deep down he admired the kid for what he'd done. He hadn't thought Ryan had that much courage in him. He thought the kid would gladly huddle in the ravine with his dad and wait for help. He never dreamed Ryan would actually take it upon himself to come walking down the road as he had.

After about 20 minutes, Ryan called out, "How far you figure we've come?"

"Great," Mike muttered under his breath. "Here it comes. The whining, the sore feet, the aching legs, the demand to stop and rest!" But Mike just called back to Ryan, "About twelve miles."

"Oh, that's pretty good, huh?" Ryan said, surprising Mike again. "That's more than halfway, huh?"

"I guess so," Mike said grudgingly. "I hope so."

At 1:00 in the morning they stopped for a rest. "Be careful where you sit," Mike warned. "I sat on a rock a ways back and got bitten by a snake."

"A snake!" Ryan gasped.

Mike showed Ryan his hand. "Here's where he got me. I thought it was a rattlesnake. I was sure I was a goner. But it turned out to be a patch-nosed snake. They aren't poisonous," he said.

"Wow," Ryan said, whistling. "If it'd been a rattler, you'd be dying or something, huh?"

"Maybe," Mike said.

"But you got lucky," Ryan said. He looked thoughtful then. "But maybe it's not luck. Maybe stuff happens for a reason. Maybe you've got something real important to do in life."

Mike smiled faintly at the other boy. "Maybe," he said.

Ryan sat on the mound of sand and said, "Know what? You look like Dad. You look just like him. Man, I'd give anything to look like him and to be like him."

Mike shrugged. "Everybody's got their good points and their bad points, I guess," he said.

A sad look came to Ryan's face. "Yeah, I guess, but when your father's in prison for doing bad stuff, you wonder how you're gonna turn out. I heard a lady say once that the apple doesn't fall far from the tree."

"That's stupid," Mike said, getting up. "Come on, let's go." Mike's legs were really tired now, and his feet hurt. He thought he was probably getting blisters, but it didn't matter. He had to keep going until he reached the highway—no matter what.

9 "Man, it's getting windy," Ryan said as they walked. Mike noticed it too, and it worried him. The desert breeze had turned into a stiff wind. Sand was rising in little puffs. Mike remembered going through New Mexico with his father once when a sandstorm blew up out of nowhere. Pretty soon visibility was down to zero. It even blotted out the sun. Sand blew all over the road and even into the closed windows of their motor home.

Mike hoped it wouldn't get that bad here.

But the wind kept picking up.

"Tie your T-shirt over your face like I'm doing," Mike told Ryan. Ryan followed suit, and they walked on. But it was getting more difficult to fight the wind. The blowing sand was making dunes, and they struggled to walk.

"Let's take a rest behind these rocks," Mike said. "Maybe the wind will die down, and we can make up the time when it's not such a struggle."

The boys huddled behind the rocks as the wind howled and the sand blew in great clouds. The moon and the stars disappeared, and the whole desert seemed in motion. Mike was terrified, but he kept silent. So, he thought bitterly, was I saved from the rattlesnake bite so I could be buried alive in a sandstorm? What was that all about?

The boys fell into a fitful sleep in their hiding place. The wind howled around them. Mike dreamed he woke up to the blazing sun bearing down on them. They knew they were doomed. Then he jumped in his sleep and woke himself up, gripped by panic. How long had they been sleeping? Was it almost morning? He was afraid to look at the watch on his wrist. "Ryan! Wake up! We gotta move fast!" he shouted.

Mike finally looked at his watch. It was 4:00! In two hours the sun would be up again!

"Come on, let's go, let's go!" Mike screamed. "We've barely got time to get to the highway. With every bit of luck on our side, we'll barely beat the sun."

Ryan scrambled to his feet. "Mike," he asked in a hollow voice, "where's the road we been following? Do you see it?"

"It's gotta be right here," Mike said, kicking at the new pattern of sand spread over the land. He knew how to find direction by following the North Star, but when he looked into the sky, the clouds of sand obscured everything. He dashed around, clawing the sand, searching for the road, but he couldn't find the tire tracks. He staggered to his feet, terror clawing at him. He didn't even know which direction was west!

Ryan started fumbling in his backpack. Suddenly he withdrew a small object. "I've got this compass. You think it'd help? I got it for my birthday when I was 12. I've never used it, but I decided to throw it into my backpack for this trip."

Mike turned sharply and grabbed it. Back when he was a boy camping with his dad, Mike always brought a compass. The only reason he didn't on this trip was that he was too affronted to do any planning.

"Is it going to help?" Ryan asked eagerly.

"Yeah," Mike said. "See, the needle points north, and that means west is to our left. Come on, let's go! It's a good thing you had it, Ryan."

The boys hurried west, moving as fast as they could over the sand. Mike stole regular nervous glances at the sky, dreading a sign of dawn.

"You sure we're going in the right direction?" Ryan asked after a little while. "I mean, that's just a cheap compass."

"Yeah, I think so," Mike said, his own confidence faltering. He didn't feel as if they were going west. Maybe his sense of direction had been scrambled.

Why didn't I bring my good compass? Mike thought to himself. Why am I such an idiot?

Mike glanced at his watch. It was almost 4:30. He was sweating heavily with fear. He was almost certain they were going in the wrong direction. He thought they were doubling back. There was almost no water left in Ryan's canteen, and they were probably hopelessly lost!

Mike suddenly dropped to his knees in the sand, despair clutching at him. "We're lost," he cried. "Your toy compass is wrong, wrong, *wrong*!" Mike felt his breath coming in painful spurts. His legs hurt so much he could scarcely move. "This is it, kid, we're doomed!"

Ryan grabbed Mike's arm. "Mike, don't give up," he pleaded. "Please don't give up. We've gotta keep going."

"Going *where*?" Mike screamed over the wind. "In circles until our hearts stop?" He yanked free of Ryan. "It's over, man!"

"Mike, the compass says north is—" Ryan began.

"Your stupid little toy compass is a cruel joke. It must be broken, if it ever did work. Leave me alone!" Mike said.

"Please, Mike, I don't want to die. Not without a fight," Ryan sobbed. "We've gotta try . . . come on," he tugged on Mike's arm, dragging the older boy to his feet. "Dad was always bragging on you, how strong and brave you were. I wanted so bad to be like you. Please don't give up on us now . . ." Tears ran down Ryan's face, smearing the sand that coated his face.

Mike stared around. Nothing looked familiar. They must have walked into the middle of the desert, far from the road that had brought them here. Mike saw a glimmer of light in the sky, the harbinger of the fiery day that would kill them. Mike stared at Ryan. Why was he yelling and crying and screaming like that? It was no use. Didn't he see that?

Couldn't he let Mike at least die in peace?

10 "All right, okay," Mike finally groaned. "We'll keep walking until we drop, if that's what you want. Yeah. We're not going anywhere, but we'll keep moving!"

They trudged on through the sand. Ryan kept looking at his compass and hoping it was accurate. "It says we're going west," he said in a desperate voice.

Mike watched the sky like you'd watch an animal that was poised to pounce on you. At first the light was barely perceptible, just a fading of the deep blackness of the sky. Then a silvery glow appeared. It was now moving closer toward the moment the burning red eye of the sun would peer over the mountains, then rise like a fiery monster. The air itself would begin to sizzle. Then there would be nowhere to go, nowhere to hide.

"What's *that*?" Ryan asked in a hushed voice.

"What?" Mike asked numbly. He had

stopped hearing anything. He had stopped feeling anything. "I didn't hear anything."

"It's like a roar," Ryan whispered.

Mike glanced at the sky. The dust clouds were almost gone. Mike figured it would make it all the easier for the rays of the sun to reach them without even a screen of dust to filter the intensity. "Probably a plane up 30,000 feet," Mike said grimly. They were probably up there drinking ice-cold colas and eating peanuts, without a clue about the awful little drama being played out on the sand below.

"Didn't sound like a plane," Ryan said stubbornly. "Sounded like . . . like . . ." He dared not form the word.

"Like what?" Mike demanded.

"A car," Ryan croaked.

They saw it then before them, the highway they had been struggling toward. It was the highway Mike had come to believe they would never find.

A car flashed by, a blue car. Then it was gone.

"Come on," Mike cried in a suddenly energized voice. "Come on!"

They started running, stumbling the last few yards to the highway. Mike dropped to his knees and cut himself on a sharp stone. The blood oozed through his jeans, but he paid no attention to it. He scrambled up and, grabbing Ryan's arm, dragged the other boy in a running, stumbling gait. They waded through the sand, kicking it up, trying to leap over the dunes. Their legs ached mercilessly, but they didn't stop.

Sand had blown across the highway, but they could still see the blacktop and the white line in the middle.

"Not much traffic on this road," Mike said, "but another car could come pretty soon." Mike was breathing hard from the last mad dash, but now he knew they would be okay. Rescue was within reach. Joy surged back into his body, enlivening him.

They waited ten minutes for another vehicle to come. They could already feel the heat, but it still wasn't oppressive. A remnant of the night's coolness remained.

Both boys stood on the side of the road waving frantically as a pickup came closer. Whoever was driving stepped on the gas and disappeared down the road.

"They probably think we're some kind of criminals trying to trick them or something," Mike said. He stripped off his T-shirt. Then he fumbled in his backpack until he found a black felt pen. He scrawled "call the police" on the back of the sweat-stained shirt.

Now without his shirt, Mike tried to huddle in the scant shade of a bullet-marked traffic sign. Mike figured kids must've used it for target practice.

Fifteen minutes later, another car came into view. Mike jumped up frantically and waved the T-shirt message. A young woman was driving. She slowed, then sped on, obviously frightened.

"Oh, man, oh, man," Mike groaned, "nobody is *ever* going to stop! We got this far, and we'll probably die out here anyway!"

"Somebody has to stop and help," Ryan said in a whimper. He sounded like a scared ten-year-old. He was losing his courage too. It was all just too much. Ryan put his face in his hands, and his shoulders convulsed with sobs.

Mike walked over and put his hand on

the other boy's shoulder. "Come on, Ryan, it'll be okay. If you hadn't gotten after me when I wanted to quit, we'd be lying out on the desert baking right now. You saved my life by forcing me to keep walking. I would have curled up in a ball and died in some sand dune a quarter of a mile from the highway, okay?" he said. "And your stupid little compass saved us too. If it hadn't been for that, we never would've found the right direction. So you got us this far, man, okay? Don't lose your grip now."

Ryan nodded and sat down, his head buried in his arms.

It was about 20 minutes more before they spotted the police car, its red lights blinking in the morning sun. The car slowed where the boys stood, and two officers peered out cautiously.

"What's going on here?" one of them asked.

"We had an accident," Mike said. "Our dad is back about 20 miles in a ravine alongside our wrecked SUV. My brother and I have been hiking out all night to get help."

The cop nodded and started asking for help on his radio. In less than 20 minutes the place was crawling with paramedics and even a helicopter.

When Mike glanced at Ryan, he noticed the boy was crying. He slapped him on the back and said, "Hey, crying time is over. We're okay, man!"

"Do you remember what you said?" Ryan asked.

"What I said? No, what'd I say?" Mike asked then.

"You said *our dad* is back about 20 miles." Ryan repeated in a halting voice. "You said *my brother and I* were hiking all night . . ."

"Did I say that?" Mike asked with a grin. He had never felt more achy and hot and miserable, nor happier in his entire life. His lips were coated with sand, and he was hoarse from the sand in his throat.

But he was alive. They were alive. They had made it.

***

At the hospital Mike embraced his father, who was found to have a badly sprained leg. He had not hugged his father in eight years.

Mike felt lighthearted, as though a burden he had been carrying for a long time had at last been lifted. He knew the burden he carried was the resentment he felt against his father. He would never forget the hurt of the past eight years, nor would he ever quite understand it. But he had been set free—he had forgiven his father at last.